F is for Football

ABC'S Book

Written by Julie Kicklighter   Illustrated by Pixel Boy Studio

A is for America's favorite sport

Can't hide that American pride.
Football's number one!

D is for Defense

Hold 'em. Defense. Hold 'em!

E is for End Zone

Our team owns the End Zone.
Raise that score!

20 ‹30

F is for Football

Dedicated to domination.
This is a Football Nation!

G is for Goalpost

G.O.A.L. Over the Goal!

I is for Interception

J is for Jersey

Hey! It's time to cheer.
Yell your color here!

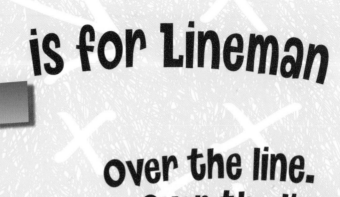

L is for Lineman

over the line.
over the line.
Go, Go, Go!

M is for Midfield

**Move that ball down the field.
Let's Go Team!**

N is for Number 1

We're number one!
Not two, not three, not four.
We're number one!

O is for Offense

offense. Get working. Let's move that ball and score!

Q is for Quarterback

Control that ball!
Our QB can do it all!

R is for Referee

Ref wears stripes,
thin & tall.

Knows the rules,
makes the call.

S is for Stadium

Whose house?
OUR HOUSE!

T is for Touchdown

Six points more.
Score! Score!

U is for Uniform

Helmet, shoulder pads,
mouth piece, cleat.

Our team
can't be beat!

W is for Whistle

Whistle blows.
It's time to GO!

Blows again.
It's time to end.

X is for X's and O's

Our team has the plays
to WIN today!

Y is for Yard Line

Team working hard!
Gain that yard!

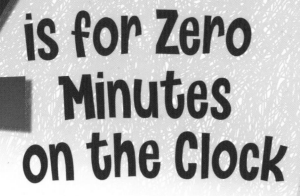

Z is for Zero Minutes on the Clock

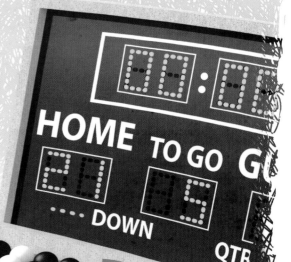

Tick tock.
Zero minutes on the clock.
Game over!

Julie Kicklighter, known as Kick by her friends and colleagues, grew up in the South with two older brothers in a family of athletes and sports enthusiasts. She followed the family tradition in her own way by becoming a cheerleader at Georgia Southern University. She went on to become a Miami Dolphins Cheerleader. She was awarded 2005 Rookie of the Year by the organization for a stand out season that included performing stand-up comedy at NFL Draft Day, Miami Dolphins Fan Fest, and performing overseas for the troops with the Armed Forces Entertainment Group.

Julie has appeared in front of the camera on Fox Sports Net, Spike TV, and the NFL Network. She has been the subject of features by Channel 10's Sports Jam Live, Channel 7's Sports Extra, and Fins TV on NBC 6. She has been heard on air on WQAM Sports Talk Radio Miami, ESPN Radio Orlando & Tampa, CBS Sports Talk Radio Tampa, and the Dolphins Fanatics Online Radio Show.

Julie is currently working as a sports model and competitor. She can be seen on workout videos with fitness gurus Denise Austin, Jennifer Nicole Lee, and Brenda Dygraf. She is also a Miami Dolphins Cheerleader Ambassador, assisting with their Youth Cheer Camps, game day fan relations, and the Miami Dolphins Special Teams (a community outreach program). Julie is also a member of Sweethearts for Soldiers, a select group of former NFL and NBA Cheerleaders who provide entertainment for the troops overseas and stateside.

Other books by Julie Kicklighter

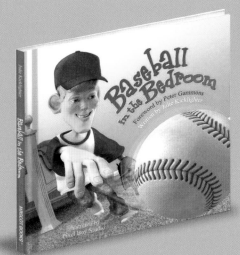

with foreword by
Peter Gammons

www.juliekicklighter.com

Pixel Boy Studio, based in Chicago, is a creative partnership between brothers Mark and Lee Fullerton. Originally from the advertising industry, their interests evolved to children's illustration and 3D animation. They've illustrated for Scholastic, Highlights, Sports Illustrated Kids, Fisher-Price, The Arizona Science Center, numerous children's educational books and many other players. Currently, the brothers are going long and diving into the E-book realm with their own original story.

Learn more at www.pixelboystudio.com